OOOPS!

Suzy Kline
pictures **by Dora Leder**

PUFFIN BOOKS

PUFFIN BOOKS
Published by the Penguin Group
Viking Penguin, a division of Penguin Books USA Inc.,
40 West 23rd Street, New York, New York 10010, U.S.A.
Penguin Books Ltd, 27 Wrights Lane, London W8 5TZ, England
Penguin Books Australia Ltd, Ringwood, Victoria, Australia
Penguin Books Canada Ltd, 2801 John Street, Markham, Ontario, Canada L3R 1B4
Penguin Books (N.Z.) Ltd, 182–190 Wairau Road, Auckland 10, New Zealand

Penguin Books Ltd, Registered Offices: Harmondsworth, Middlesex, England

First published in the United States of America by Albert Whitman & Company, 1988
Published in Picture Puffins 1989
1   3   5   7   9   10   8   6   4   2

LIBRARY OF CONGRESS CATALOGING-IN-PUBLICATION DATA
Kline, Suzy   Ooops! / Suzy Kline ; pictures by Dora Leder.   p.   cm.
Summary: An energetic preschooler who often drops and spills
things feels relieved when she notices the adults around her
occasionally having their share of mishaps.
ISBN 0-14-050986-0
[1. Clumsiness—Fiction.]   I. Leder, Dora , ill.   II. title.
[PZ7.K67970o 1989]   [E]—dc20   89-32424

Printed in Hong Kong by South China Printing Co.

For my Emmy Sue *S.K.*
For my nephew, Wyatt   *D.L.*

Ooops . . . I dropped my soap.

Uh oh . . . the towel fell in.

Ooops . . . I spilled my juice.

HELP! It splashed on Dad.

Ooops . . . my coat slid off.

Uh oh . . . it knocked down Joe's.

Ooops . . . I tripped on the cat. Oh boy!

Now *how*
did I
do that?

Mom says, "Be careful!"

Dad says, "Slow down!"

But I am not the *only* one
who does an ooops around.

Ooops . . . Mom dropped the phone.
Uh oh . . . it was her boss.

Ooops . . . Dad ripped the bag.

LOOK OUT! There go the eggs!

Ooops . . . the teacher dribbled paint.

Oh, no! On the *principal!*

Ooops . . . Mom slipped on ice.
Uh oh . . . she did it twice!

Ooops . . . Dad dropped his glasses.
Oh boy! There goes a lens!

It seems to me
it's not just me

that does an Ooops

occasionally.

See?
Most of the time
I do just fine!